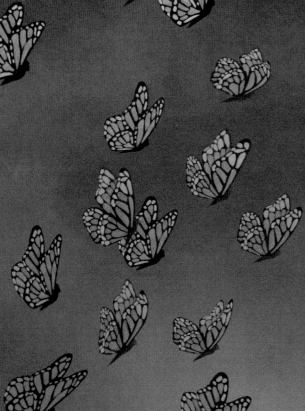

This book belongs to:

☺ Madison ♡

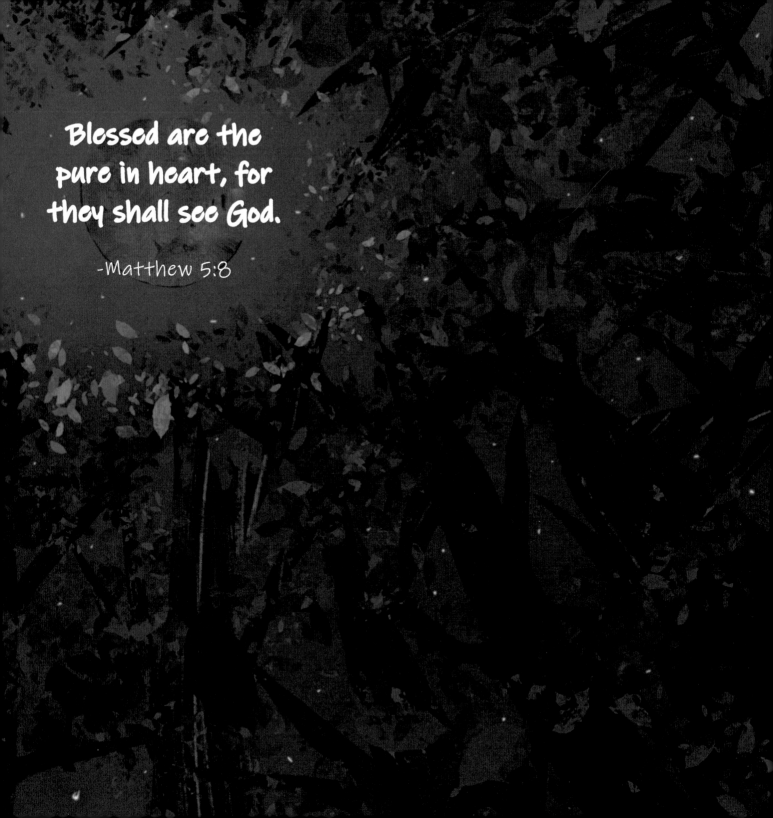

Blessed are the
pure in heart, for
they shall see God.

-Matthew 5:8

The illustrations for this book were created using painted paper collage and rendered digitally.

Cataloging-in-Publication Data is available from the Library of Congress.
Library of Congress Control Number: 2023902931

ISBN
Hardcover: 978-1-7374300-3-2
Paperback: 978-1-7374300-2-5

Published by Iris Arc Press
First Edition

For You
- K.G.

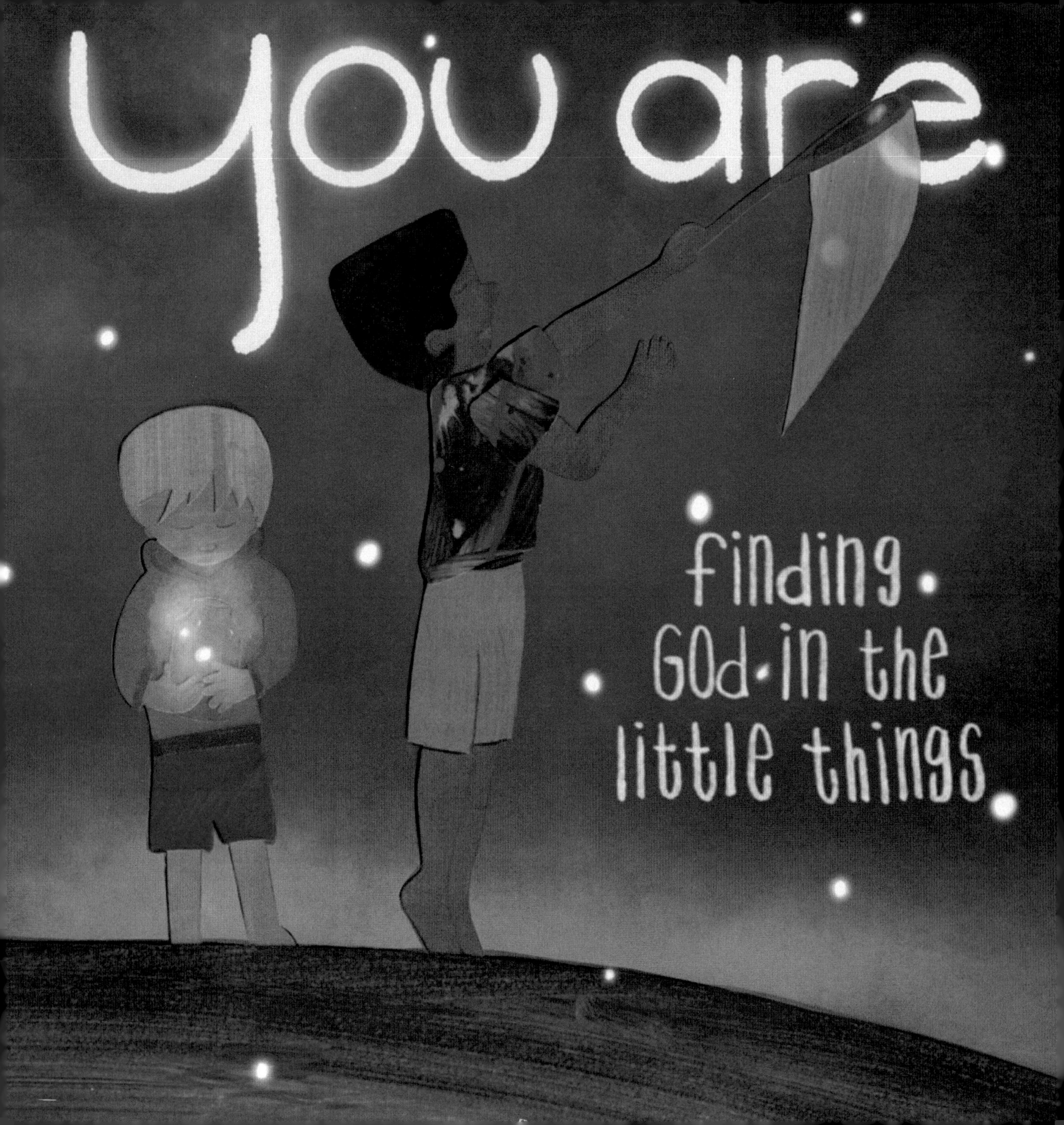
you are
finding God in the little things

When my mind feels very messy
and I don't know what is best;
I come to **You** with worries and
**Your** word assures me rest.

I close my eyes so tightly and
take a breath or two;
and then I am aware of things
that bring me close to **You**.

I see **You** in the
sunrise and in the
dazzling dew;

in blooming buds in springtime, as life begins anew.

**Your** gentle hand, it guides me, along each merry mile.

**You** pave the path to follow with a sweet and caring smile.

**Your** joy is felt in raindrops, and in the bright, warm sun;

in crashing waves
around us and in
friends all having fun.

**Your** giving heart provides me
with patience, peace and love.

You faithfully restore me
as I hear Your voice above.

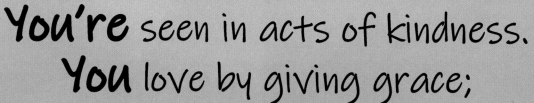

You're seen in acts of kindness.
YOU love by giving grace;

and when I'm weak
and weary, **You're**
the comforting
embrace.

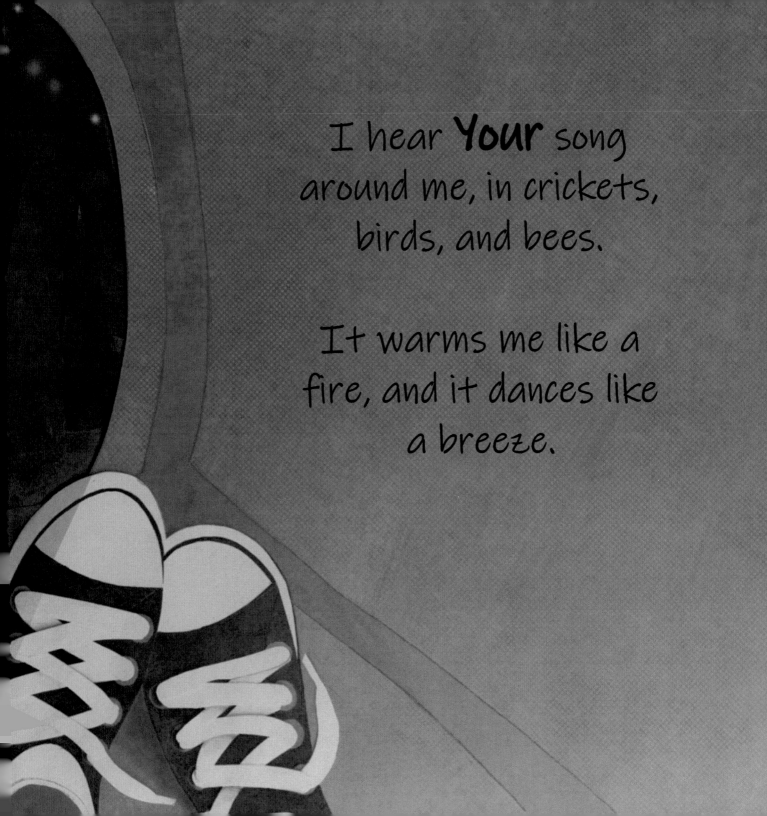

I hear **Your** song around me, in crickets, birds, and bees.

It warms me like a fire, and it dances like a breeze.

You're calm,
like fresh snow
falling upon a
still dark
night;

and like the cold **You're** quiet, but **Your** mercy still shines bright.

**You** know
my heartfelt
longings; the
answer to my
prayer.

**You** are my
loving savior,
and **You're**

# simply
## EVERYWHERE!

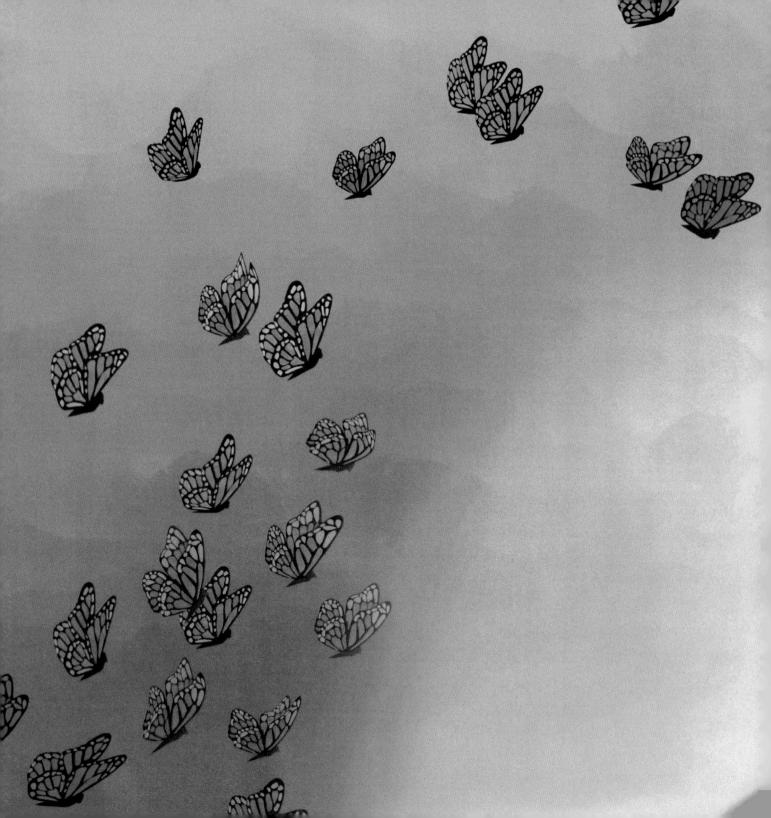

## Authors Note:

Throughout history, butterflies have been
symbolic of many things. Peace, transformtion, comfort,
hope, beauty, and love to name a few. Included on the pages
of this book are many butterflies. How many can you find?
They are one of the many ways God reveals himself.
How will you find God in the little things today?

You will seek Me and find Me when you search for Me with all your heart.

-Jeremiah 29:13

Made in the USA
Middletown, DE
30 June 2023

34298900R00024